Big Dog and Little Dog

Going for a Walk

Dav Pilkey

Houghton Mifflin Harcourt
Boston New York

www.hmhco.com

Library of Congress Cataloging-in-Publication Data is on file.
ISBN 978-0-544-43072-3 paper over board
ISBN 978-0-544-43071-6 paperback

Manufactured in China
SCP 10 9 8 7 6 5 4 3 2 1

4500521216

Ages	Grades	Guided Reading Level	Reading Recovery Level	Lexile® Level
4–6	K	D	5–6	350L

To Nathan Douglas Libertowski

Big Dog is going for a walk.

Little Dog is going, too.

Little Dog likes to play in the mud.

Big Dog likes to eat the mud.

Little Dog likes to splash
in the puddles.

Big Dog likes to drink the puddles.

Big Dog and Little Dog
had a fun walk.

They are very dirty.

It is time to take a bath.

Big Dog and Little Dog
are in the tub.

Now it is time to dry off.

Big Dog and Little Dog
shake and shake.

Big Dog and Little Dog
are clean and dry.

Now they want to go for
another walk.

Cause and Effect

What goes up must come down—every cause has an effect! Here is one from the story:

Cause: Big Dog and Little Dog play in mud.

Effect: Big Dog and Little Dog get dirty.

Can you think of any other causes and effects from the story?

Picture It

Read the sentences below.
Can you match them with the correct image?

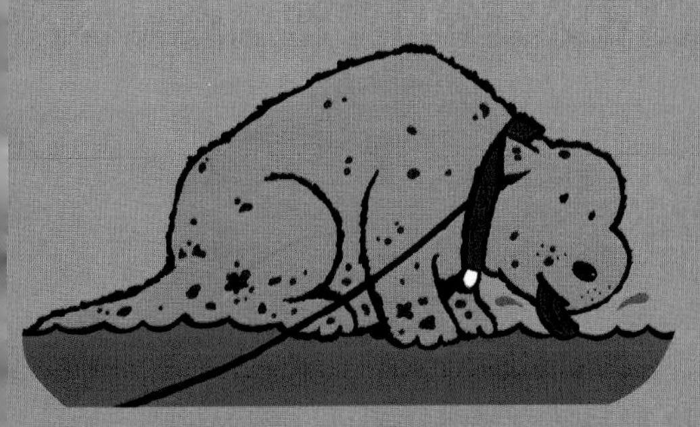

Big Dog and Little Dog are in the tub.

Little Dog likes to play in the mud.

Big Dog likes to drink the puddles.

Big Dog and Little Dog are going for a walk.

Story Sequencing

The story of Big Dog and Little Dog going for a walk got scrambled! Can you put the scenes in the right order?

Doggone amazing!

Can you believe these dog facts?

- A greyhound can run as fast as forty-five miles an hour.
- The beagle and collie are the noisiest dogs. The Akbash dog and the basenji are the quietest.
- President Lyndon Johnson had two beagles named Him and Her.
- The United States has more dogs than any other country in the world.
- The expression "the dog days of summer" goes back to ancient Roman times, when people thought Sirius, the dog star, created heat on Earth.
- Dog nose prints are as unique as human fingerprints—no two dog noses are alike.

Drawing Dogs

Big Dog and Little Dog love to go for walks.
What other adventures do you think they go on?

On a seperate sheet of paper, draw your own pictures of Big Dog and Little Dog doing things and going places! Here are some ideas to get you started:

Big Dog and Little Dog learn a new trick.

Big Dog and Little Dog play fetch.

Big Dog and Little Dog ride in a car.

Big Dog and Little Dog howl at the moon.

Canine Comedy

Try these jokes on your friends!
Can you think of any other dog jokes?

Q: What do you say when your dog does something great?

A: Pawsome!

Q: What do dogs have that no other animal has?

A: Puppies.

Q: What kind of dog can use the phone?

A: A dial-mation.

Q: Why is a tree like a big dog?

A: They both have a lot of bark.

Q: Which animal keeps the best time?

A: A watch dog.